Ace and the Misfits

Ace and the Misfits

Eddie Kawooya

James Lorimer & Company Ltd., Publishers
Toronto

James Lorimer & Company Ltd., Publishers acknowledges funding support from the Ontario Arts Council (OAC), an agency of the Government of Ontario. We acknowledge the support of the Canada Council for the Arts. This project has been made possible in part by the Government of Canada and with the support of Ontario Creates.

Cover design: Tyler Cleroux
Cover image: iStock, Shutterstock

Library and Archives Canada Cataloguing in Publication

Title: Ace and the misfits / Eddie Kawooya.
Names: Kawooya, Eddie, author.
Identifiers: Canadiana (print) 20230229360 | Canadiana (ebook) 20230229379 | ISBN 9781459417526 (hardcover) | ISBN 9781459417519 (softcover) | ISBN 9781459417533 (EPUB)
Classification: LCC PS8621.A772 A65 2024 | DDC jC813/.6—dc23

Published by:
James Lorimer & Company
Ltd., Publishers
117 Peter Street, Suite 304
Toronto, ON, Canada
M5V 0M3
www.lorimer.ca

Distributed in Canada by:
Formac Lorimer Books
5502 Atlantic Street
Halifax, NS, Canada
B3H 1G4
www.formaclorimerbooks.ca

Distributed in the US by:
Lerner Publisher Services
241 1st Ave. N.
Minneapolis, MN, USA
55401
www.lernerbooks.com

Printed and bound in Canada.

Contents

This book is dedicated to the many journalists in Uganda and the East African region who put their lives on the line to report on crucial and significant stories. It is also dedicated to organizations like the Journalists for Human Rights that work to help develop and train journalists across the African continent to tell our stories.

CHAPTER 1
SOME NEWS TO SHARE

Kind words do not wear out the tongue.

– Liberian proverb

A few inches taller and none the wiser, the now twelve-year-old Patrick "Ace" Katumba could feel the rush of adrenaline coursing through his legs. Ace was the nickname his mom gave him, not particularly for his sports skills, but after a Ugandan comic book hero, *The Fearless Night Ace,* whom Ace admired and dressed up as when he was young.

He had to set aside all his fears and worries to make it happen. Ace pushed himself off the ground as high as he could, twisting his entire body like a figure skater. He stretched out his left foot, and with all his might volleyed the soccer ball into the opposing team's net.

As soon as he landed back on his feet, he heard the cries of victory flooding the soccer grounds. Ace's teammates rushed to pick him up from the grass and carry him on their shoulders.

"We won! Your leaping dragon kick finally paid off!" shouted one of the boys.

"Manchester United can keep its players! Kampala has its Ace!" screamed another.

Ace for his part roared to the crowds and pointed at Zzabu, his mother, a stylishly bespectacled, forty-something woman with glowing brown skin in a matching jeans uniform, and his sister, Olive, who was tall, slender, had golden-coloured braids, and dressed in all white.

"Ace, Ace, he's our man! Ace, Ace, show them all!" the crowds chanted gleefully.

The chanting and cheers continued right up to the award ceremony where the city's mayor, a fancily dressed middle-aged man with greying hair and rich ebony skin, got to present the trophy and take pictures with the winning team. The mayor quickly pulled Ace to his side and shook the young man's hand like he had just solved the problem of world hunger.

"Superstar!" the mayor yelled. "How does it feel to be a champion? We all want to know, Ace! We all want to know your secret!"

Ace's sense of joy and excitement quickly fell, replaced by fear and anxiety.

"I ... I ..." Ace trembled as the words failed to come out of his mouth.

"Superstar!" shouted the mayor again. *"ACE! ACE!"*

Before he heard his name being called again, Ace felt the cold splash of water hit his face. He opened his eyes to see two people standing above him with a look of concern. He was daydreaming again. It had become more frequent since his father's passing. The dreams were always different but provided a reality free from the anxiety and secrets he bore alone.

"Wake up, sleepyhead," said Rodney, a short and scruffy boy covered in dirt and mud. "We're losing the match and you are here daydreaming. Get up already!"

"Get away, Rodney!" screamed Ronan, a towering figure with a defined athletic build. "Aren't you the one that kicked the ball off his head with your two left feet?" He bent down to Ace's level and showed two fingers. "Ace, we need you to get up and score two more goals before the lunch bell rings. We'll take you to the school nurse afterward, and you can daydream there, okay?"

"Two ... two ... goals," Ace said weakly as he brought himself up from the ground. He suddenly realized that he was in his school uniform: short-sleeved white dress shirt, navy blue tie and navy shorts, and black shoes.

"Yes, Ace! Okay, people. The superstar is back! Someone tell the Grade 6 kids to collect some tissues for their tears, after our Grade 7 team wins. Let's go, Ace!" Rodney insisted.

"I really don't feel so great ... I need to sit down for a

bit," Ace said while touching his bruised head.

"Rodney, this is the last time we let you do free kicks. We've lost three players already this semester, and now we're about to lose our fourth player and star striker. Treat that ball like you do your math homework — run away!" Ronan gestured at Rodney.

"Flap your gums again, Ronan, and I'll use my two left feet to drop-kick you! I've taken out four players. Don't tempt me with a fifth!" Rodney smirked, raising his palm with all five fingers stretched out.

"Oh, you wanna go now!" Ronan said, about to pounce on Rodney before Ace stood between them.

"Ronan … Rodney." Ace looked at his friends. "Can we go sit somewhere? I'm a bit dizzy."

"Like right now? How about we win the match and then sit down?" Rodney suggested.

"Rodney!" Ronan slapped the back of Rodney's head.

"Don't tell me you're happy we're losing two nothing to the Grade 6 crew. They're literally afraid of the ball. Whatever, man, we can move Ace to the bench over there." Rodney pointed at a nearby wooden seat where some girls had been playing.

* * *

At the bench, Ronan handed Ace his bottled water. "Bro, what's happening to you today?"

12

"Just today?" Rodney blurted. "Talk about the semester. This guy used to be the top of the class, but even Sleepy Fred has better grades. Ace, you won't come and play PlayStation on the weekends. We aren't winning because we don't have our star striker. Tell us the truth. Have you joined the basketball crew? We won't get mad. I promise."

"What's wrong with the basketball crew? My brother plays with them," Ronan responded, sounding annoyed.

"Need I say more? Your brother couldn't catch a ball to save his life," Rodney said with a smirk.

"Bro, you're just jealous because your short self couldn't make the cut," Ronan replied.

"They can't handle my short-king energy!" Rodney said while beating his chest.

"I guess the Grades 5 and 6 have you handled, seeing as we keep losing when you're on the field, short king!" Ronan chuckled.

A smile appeared on Ace's face, but it was short-lived. He sighed deeply, which grabbed the attention of Ronan and Rodney.

"There's something I have to tell you both," started Ace. "Something I've been keeping a secret for too long, and I can't anymore." Ace sighed again.

"Sweet mahogany, he joined the basketball crew! I knew it!" Rodney jumped off the bench dramatically.

Ronan rolled his eyes. "Rodney, quit being a fool and let him finish."

Ace laughed loudly. "I'm going to miss you both a lot."

"What do you mean, Ace?" Ronan asked.

Rodney groaned. "Oh man, not again. The last time he got like this was before the Christmas school play. The guy had only one line but he froze like a popsicle and fainted in front of everyone. Please don't tell us you're freaking out about another class presentation?"

"Were you raised in a bush, Rodney? Shut up and let the man talk. Ace, please continue and ignore the short king."

"I'm not supposed to say anything, but my mom is moving my sister and I to Canada. I don't know why exactly. She just said with Dad gone, it'd be safer for us … That she could support us better there than in Uganda. We'll be staying with my Uncle Jackson somewhere called Toronto. You can't say anything, okay? If anyone asks, tell them she got a new job or something over there …"

Ace stopped to look at his friends' blank faces.

"So …" Rodney gestured with his hands.

"So … We'll be moving to Canada this June," confirmed Ace. "My mom is going to let the school know closer to the date. She doesn't want anyone to know. Olive and I also can't go visiting like we used to. My mom wants us to focus on our books this semester. I think it's stupid," Ace finished sadly.

"I don't get it, man," Ronan said. "You're one of the best in our grade when it comes to all the classes, even math and science. Parents can be dumb sometimes. I think they just don't like it when we have fun. I'm sorry, Ace."

"This sucks, man. It's worse than joining the stupid basketball crew!" Ronan cried. "How long will you be gone for?"

"I don't know, man. My mom just told us that Canada is going to be our new home. She said it was something my dad and her wanted before he passed away. I don't know if I'll be back to visit at all."

"Whatever happens, there will always be a place for you here, Ace. I don't care where you are in the world — you'll always be our friend. Those Canadians better get ready for the tornado called Ace!" Ronan chuckled with a couple of tears on his cheeks.

"Ace?" Rodney asked. "Are you still dizzy, or are you ready to win us this game before the lunch bell?"

Ace smiled. "I think we can turn this game around now."

"That's what I'm talking about! Oi! Grade 6 crew, get ready to shed some tears. We have our Ace card, a.k.a. Tornado Ace, back on the field!"

CHAPTER 2
POLITE & NICE

Do not lean on a wall that is not near you.

— Ghanaian proverb

It was the first Tuesday of September and the day after the Labour Day long weekend, the last long weekend of the summer. It was also the first day of the new school year, and a scorcher of a morning when Ace, Olive, and Uncle Jackson left their townhouse home near the Regent Park Area.

Ever since he could remember, Ace dreaded the first day of school in Kampala after the holidays: having to wake up before the sun rose and chickens crowed, dress in a dull uniform, endure hours of traffic only to arrive late and be reminded of holiday homework that was hardly touched because video games took priority. The lunch served was tasteless and barely passed for food.

But Ace was in Toronto now, and he welcomed the

start of the school year after spending summer doing everything fun under the sun with his family.

"Looking fresh, young sir," Uncle Jackson said, noting Ace's clean-cut hair, green camouflage T-shirt, light blue jeans, and brand-new Nike Jordans — a gift from his uncle and aunt, Annabelle.

"Now that you mention it, Uncle, he doesn't look like an angry village bushman anymore," Olive jested as she rocked her new afro, white jeans and sky-blue dress shirt with a matching blue backpack.

"Olive." Ace stopped his sister and gestured as if he was making a phone call. "It's the nineties calling … What's that? … Yes. Yes, of course. We can do that … Hey, Olive, they want their style back."

"I'm going to kick this villager!" Olive threatened. Uncle Jackson immediately held her back, chuckling.

"We can fight to the death later. We'll miss our streetcar. You both have your PRESTO cards?" Uncle Jackson asked as he grabbed a black and green card from his beige pants. He pointed at the oncoming red and white train-like vehicle, no bigger than a bus, that hovered on its special tracks etched into the ground of Queen Street East.

The streetcar looked like a caterpillar, divided into different sections, with big, open windows and powered by electricity. The car's doors automatically opened, not only to let people off but also let new ones board. One needed only to tap their card on the tiny green machine they called a PRESTO box, which confirmed payment. The interior was like an endless moving hallway with enough seats for everyone.

Ace took so much joy and wonder from riding the streetcar. It was like living in one of those high-tech societies in the movies. Public transportation in Kampala was nothing short of chaos-level busy, and almost always a near-death experience. The main means of public transport were either the matatu, a mini-bus taxi, or a motorbike taxi. Imagine a real-life *Grand Theft Auto*, where drivers scale the roads recklessly and with no concern for their passengers. You'd be lucky not to be thrown out of a moving car and into traffic if you ever forgot to pay your fare or thought of telling off the driver for their reckless driving.

Ace whispered to himself, "This is really happening!" Never in his wildest dreams did he think he would live and visit any place outside of Uganda. He dreamt about what it would be like to attend a school in New York, Los Angeles, Cape Town, or even London where they filmed his favourite TV shows and movies.

In his dreams, Ace saw himself walking confidently through the hallways, soccer ball in hand, the cheers of countless students chanting his name, teachers fist-bumping him while calling him "the man," a squad of athletes following right behind him. They loved him. They *adored* him. He was the cool kid on the block —

"Ace, stop with the daydreaming again and get your butt onto the streetcar!" hollered Uncle Jackson as he gestured for Ace to make his way into the car.

Olive had managed to find them a four-seat section of the streetcar. She looked excited to finally have a seat near a window to view the city in the morning. Ace was relieved to be out of the house after spending the last three months settling into the new city and going on hiking trips with Uncle Jackson and Aunt Annabelle. Hiking: a concept that still remained foreign to Ace and his sister.

"You look nervous, young sir," Uncle Jackson commented as he noticed Ace tightly closing his hands into fists while staring at the other passengers walking through the car.

"Who, me?" Ace asked in surprise.

"Who else am I staring at? What's up?" Uncle Jackson asked.

"I ... I ... I don't know what to expect, Uncle. Will we get in trouble for not doing any holiday homework? I've never been to a school with kids ... who are white, Chinese, or come from other cultures. Is it easy to make friends here?" asked Ace.

"Holidays are for fun and relaxation, young man. There's no holiday homework you should concern yourself with," Uncle Jackson replied before chuckling. "But I've been where you are. I came to Canada a long time ago, way before your mother had you both. I was the first in our family to win a scholarship and study abroad at the University of Toronto. I knew nothing about Canada other than what they shared in the textbook. No one told me what to expect.

"When I arrived, like you, I was stunned to see so many people of colour and white people in one city. Fortunately, there was an International Students Center at the university. This was where I made many friends from India, Pakistan, Mexico, and Nigeria who had also come from afar to study in Canada. The more I got to spend time with these people, the more I learned, and the more open my mind became.

"I realized they are just like you and I, with a slight difference in the colour of our skins and where we are from. Like you, they want friends, they want to be happy, they want to take care of their families, and they want to show love. There is nothing to worry about, young sir. Give them a chance and just be you, okay?" Uncle Jackson concluded, winking at Ace.

"I can do that, Uncle. I can do it," said Ace, nodding vigorously.

* * *

It was nine in the morning when they arrived at the door of the school, an uninspiring building modeled as a series of cubes put together with a playground near its entrance and protected by a short black metal fence. A few decorative paintings were plastered on the fence and the walls.

Uncle Jackson escorted Olive and Ace to the administrative office, a few minutes from the entrance. An older tanned man wearing a yellow tie, long brown pants, and a dress shirt with sleeves rolled up greeted the trio while grabbing a coffee.

"Hey there, how can I help ya!" said the man in a very jolly tone.

"Hey," replied Uncle Jackson, releasing Ace's shoulder to shake the man's hand. "My name is Jackson Mukono, and I am here to drop off my niece and nephew, Olive and Patrick Katumba, for the first day of class. I was in touch with the admin last week."

"Oh yes! The kids from Uganda! Welcome to Carter Parker Public School. I'll have you know that my wife and I spent some time in Uganda a few years ago. Amazing place, beautiful people, and love, *love* the food. I'm vegan these days, but I tell my wife I wouldn't mind putting that on pause to try some of those dishes again!" The man burst out laughing.

"Thank you, sir. So I can leave them in your capable hands," Uncle Jackson said as he slowly walked backward and waved goodbye to his niece and nephew.

"Goodness, I haven't even introduced myself yet. No need for sir here. I'm Principal Keller. What are your preferred names?"

"I'm Olive."

"I'm Patrick, but I prefer Ace."

"Wonderful! Ace and Olive, welcome to your first day of school. If you wait right here, I'll grab hold of your schedules and take you over to your first class." Principal Keller put down his mug and moved to speak with an administrative person close by.

As soon as they had dropped Olive off at her first class of the day, Grade 11 English, Ace was taken up a gallery of stairs to the highest point of the school for his first class, Grade 8 Art.

The class door was odd, to say the least. The handle was coloured in gold, and the door itself was painted a lime green, a stark contrast against the other class doors, which were all blue. As everyone walked into the big classroom filled with spacious desks and art materials scattered all around, they all fell silent upon seeing Principal Keller.

"Principal Keller, to what do we owe this surprise?" said the teacher.

"Ah, Ms. Reid, I wanted to introduce the class to a new student joining our school. His name is Patrick Katamba, but he prefers to go by 'Ace.' He's come all this way from Uganda. Please welcome him properly!" Principle Keller said cheerfully, not realizing he'd butchered Ace's last name.

"Welcome, Ace!" Ms. Reid said in a sweet and upbeat voice. Her curly brown hair was tied in a puffy ponytail and she wore green horn-rimmed glasses with a flowery dress. "My name is Katia Reid, but you can call me Ms. Reid. Why don't you take a seat in the back with Dwayne, Lutti and Ericksen! Guys, make some space for Ace!" She pointed to a large beige table at the back of the class, where the group of three boys sat next to each other.

Dwayne was dressed in a black and purple Toronto Raptors jersey, a matching cap worn backward, black baggy jeans, and purple sneakers. He got up to give Ace a fist bump.

"Solid," Ace said with a smile, recognizing a familiar feeling and spark when he fist-bumped Dwayne. It was almost as if he was greeting Ronan and Rodney.

"I'm Dwayne, but my real friends call me King because I rule at any video game or board game. On my left is South Africa's finest, Lutti. We like to call him Trivia 'cause he's always spitting some random facts. I think he makes them up half the time," Dwayne the King said cheerfully.

"He's jealous because he's unread and unpolished. For the last time, King, I rebuke your 'Trivia' nickname. I'd prefer 'Southern African Prince,'" said Trivia. He was short and chubby and rocked a flat-top haircut, a silver-tinted sweater and white shoes. "What do you think, Ace? Did you know that Namibia has one the largest concentrations of rock art in Africa?"

"I forgot to mention," Dwayne continued, "Trivia's mom makes him read the thesaurus every night before he goes to bed. He may throw some big words at you just to make himself look smart. Don't ask me why. Anyway, finally to my right and hailing from the land of Vikings, Denmark, is our boy Ericksen, the 'Tower.' He may look tough, but he's a teddy bear. He'd rather draw you a picture than throw a punch," Dwayne explained.

"King, we've been through this before. I'm an artist and not a Viking. Pleased to meet you, Ace. Welcome to our little United Nations." Tower stretched out his long arm to fist bump Ace as well. Ace noticed his dirty blond hair, the large Sony wireless headphones he wore around his neck, and his outfit of khaki shorts with white Adidas runners.

As Ace got himself seated, he could feel the eyes of his classmates locked on to him like hunters waiting on their prey.

"Everyone!" yelled Ms. Reid in a less joyful tone. "Quit staring and listen up! I'm going to give you all five minutes to think about your summer vacation and what you loved most about it. Five minutes, all right? If you need to stretch your legs, now's the time."

As soon as she finished speaking, a horde of students rushed over to Ace's table. One boy in particular, the one all the girls seemed to like and looked like a Swedish teen pop star, walked up to Ace with his right hand out as if to throw him a high-five. He wore an Arsenal soccer jersey and carried himself with high esteem and self-importance.

"So you're from Africa, eh? Is it true people in Africa live with wild animals?" the boy asked.

"No, who told—"

"Do you have buildings or stay in grass huts? You guys have internet, right?" The boy continued with his strange questions.

"Yo, Jamie! Ever hear of Google? You should try it sometime. It may help cure your ignorance," Dwayne jumped in.

Jamie sneered while throwing a mean look at Dwayne. "You think you're funny, eh, Dwayne! Why don't you search for something fresh to say? Oh wait, will mommy and daddy be able to afford it? Listen here, Africa, when you're ready to leave this geek squad, hang with some cool folks, hit me up. The name's Jamie Bishop."

As Jamie walked away, Dwayne turned to Ace. "Stay away from that guy, fam. Take it from us, Jamie is trouble."

More students passed by to greet and ask Ace questions. Ace was surprised to see so many students not listen to their teacher's instructions and freely do as they pleased. In Uganda, such acts of defiance were an invitation for most teachers to dole out blows with their favourite bamboo sticks, shoes, or books. The Canadian kids had no fear. *Such bravery,* Ace thought to himself.

For the first time in months, Ace felt excitement answering his classmates' questions and hearing girls giggle at his accent. He felt wanted, respected, and admired. He didn't want to let go of this moment and feeling.

"Five minutes are up, people!" Ms. Reid announced. "Let's get back to business before class ends."

When the class ended and the morning bell for the next class rang, the students packed up and bolted out of the classroom.

Ace attempted to grab the attention of his new art class friends, but to his surprise, none of the same people acknowledged his existence except Dwayne, Lutti, and Ericksen, who were kind enough to help him find his next class. Puzzled by the sheer coldness of his other classmates, Ace figured it could only be one thing: *classes must be so hard on these people that they forget where or who they are with.*

CHAPTER 3

MEMORIES

However far a stream flows, it never forgets its source.

— Ugandan proverb

BEEP! BEEP! BEEP!

"Ace! Wake the heck up already! Get your butt out of bed, we're going to be late!" shouted Olive, still dressed in her magenta PJs, as she rocked her brother from his slumber.

"Pass the ball, Ronaldo … Pass the bloody ball," Ace said with his eyes closed, undisturbed by his sister's pleas.

SPLASH!

"WH … WHAT … What the hell, Olive!" Ace yelled after Olive splashed a glass of cold water onto his face and pillow.

"Get in the shower. You overslept again!" said Olive with her arms folded.

"C–can you give me a minute … What's that smell …

The beeping?" It took Ace a little longer to notice the smoke coming from the kitchen area and his mother rustling with plates and pans. "Please don't tell me it happened again," he said with a hint of sorrow.

"Yup, Mom made her classic burning man breakfast. We'd be better off using Uncle Jackson's grill at this point," Olive said sarcastically.

"OLIVE! Is your brother in the shower? I don't hear the water running. ACE! You better be showering or else those buttocks of yours will be feeling my fire!" Their mom's stern voice could be heard through the thin walls.

"Yes, Mama," Ace said as he sped past Olive and jumped into the small mustard-coloured bathroom.

Just like that, Ace's daily routine had kicked off. A hostile awakening from an unbearable and possibly possessed sister. The jury was still out on that one. A quick ten-minute shower before a sleep-deprived mother knocked on the door to fuss about eating breakfast: a burned omelette and oat porridge. Sprinkle honey and ketchup on said breakfast in hopes it might magically taste better, at least better than it looked. Realize honey and ketchup don't do the trick. Rush out of the door with Ziploc®-packed sandwiches with hopes of catching the 8:15 streetcar to school. They always missed that streetcar.

"It feels good to be out of that dungeon." Olive sighed deeply as they waited for the next streetcar to show.

The pair had on matching sweaters their mother had gotten for them from Walmart, except Ace's was grey and Olive's was a bright pink bubblegum colour.

"If you weren't taking your sweet ol' time, we could have been out sooner. It's so dark in that house sometimes," Ace complained.

"It's called a basement apartment, dummy. Basement being the key word. Uncle Jackson is renting it to us for free until Mom can get a job and we can move into our own place," Olive explained.

"Are all houses in Toronto like this? Small and cramped? Even the smallest of houses in Kampala have a garden and enough space to move around inside. This is a strange place, sis," said Ace, taking a mental note of their small basement apartment unit. Located below street level, the house had laminate flooring, a large enough living room, a kitchen island, one shared bathroom, and three bedrooms.

It was during the same month of September that Ace noticed the days get shorter, the air chillier, and the colour of the leaves morph from welcoming emerald green to rust-coloured orange.

As the season moved forward, Ace's mind raced back in time, back to Kampala. He missed laughing at and with the mischievous Rodney, whose not-so-well-planned pranks landed him at the principal's office. He missed Ronan's level-headed attitude toward everything and always knowing just what to say at the right moment. He missed his friends.

What Ace missed most of all was his football, or *soccer* as it was called in Canada. It all came back to him. The rush he got just kicking the ball, dribbling it across the field, playing tricks with the goalkeeper before scoring a goal, and having the team cheer him on. He missed it all.

Uncle Jackson had actually encouraged Ace to sign up for the Grade 8 soccer team, but he shied away from doing so. In Uganda, he had Rodney and Ronan to encourage him. In Canada, he felt self-conscious and alone.

Even if he wanted to, his mom was not supportive. When he brought up the idea with her to buy some soccer cleats, she reminded him in a very strict tone: "This is not Kampala, Ace. We do not have time to be playing games. Football is not going to pay for university. You're at school to receive a good education and head to a top school. If you can show me good grades, then we can talk. Until then, I want you to focus on your books."

At least school meant having the freedom to see daylight and escape his family's home.

"Hey, idiot," Olive whispered to her brother.

"Hey, tall neck," Ace replied.

"Isn't that kiddo with baggy pants in your grade? The skinny one with a Raptors cap and black and gold jersey?" Olive gestured with her mouth — because it was rude to point in Ugandan culture — at the boy who shared the same ebony complexion as her and Ace.

It was none other than Dwayne the King. He must have lived nearby to be catching the same streetcar to school.

Dwayne caught Ace's eyes and gestured before walking over to him.

"'Sup, fam! You still 'round this block?" He fist-bumped Ace while acknowledging Olive.

"Yeah, really close to here. I didn't know this was your hood too!" Ace said.

"My pops actually lives here in Regent Park and my mom over in High Park. They're separated, so I spend a few days here and the rest with my mom. This your sis? You don't look alike, bro. I can see who got the good looks," Dwayne said in a charming tone.

Olive smirked and rolled her eyes. "Hey, I'm Olive and aliens abducted my brother and replaced him with what you have here. That'd explain the looks department."

"Don't encourage her like that, man. We haven't had the chance to show her what she really looks like in the mirror," Ace quipped, dodging Olive's soft jab. "Where's Lutti and Ericksen?"

"They're at soccer tryouts this morning. I'll be heading to the afternoon tryouts. We didn't get in last year, but this is our year. You play ball, Ace? Please say yes. Lutti couldn't direct his feet to kick a ball in a straight line. Come kick it with us after school?" Dwayne insisted.

In his heart of hearts, Ace wanted to say *yes*. He wanted to join in and just kick the ball again, but he couldn't muster up the courage.

"I'll see, man. I just have tons of homework, and would have to ask my mom. Next time, maybe."

"No sweat, bro. I'll see you in the Art room. Nice meeting you, Olive the beautiful!"

Ace said no more as he heard the ringing red and white streetcar come to a halt to pick up passengers. It was already packed with people — hardly a place to continue the conversation. A relief for Ace. He did not want to be reminded of what he could not have, and wanted the most: the chance to play soccer again.

* * *

Ace hoped that a few weeks into school, things would begin to feel normal. Or as normal as they could get. Like the American high school shows and movies he'd eagerly watched in Uganda, he hoped to relate with classmates more and even get in on the inside jokes. He hoped the feeling of being lonely, the feeling of being left out, would go away. It didn't.

In Art class, there was of course Dwayne, Lutti, and Ericksen whom Ace enjoyed sitting and talking with about the English Premier League and their favourite players. The trio was so close, Ace didn't know whether they'd welcome a fourth person to their squad. There was also Jamie Bishop, though Jamie rarely acknowledged Ace or showed any interest in anything other than drawing attention to his own life updates.

"You're telling me that you have power blackouts in Uganda happening, like, every day? And that you have to boil your water every time?" Jamie dramatically exclaimed, as if Ace was some important discovery that needed to be shared. "Oh man, I'm so blessed to be born in Canada. I mean, I don't know if I would be able to survive there … Whatever, not my problem. You guys heard the news, right? I made the Grade 8 soccer team!"

Every interaction had to start and end with Jamie talking about himself. Unlike Dwayne the King, Ace didn't know what to say with Jamie. He just bit his tongue and nodded to whatever Jamie, *Mr. Popular*, said.

In Science class, there was of course Tim Chung, honest and direct. He was a few inches taller than Ace, with fair features, black hair, and glasses. He always had a pair of Noir Sony headphones around his neck, just like Ericksen, Tower. If you ever wanted an honest opinion about something, you'd go to Tim.

He once made a classmate cry after she asked his opinion of her new glasses. He told her she looked like a grandmother. He apologized afterward and suggested a store that sold glasses that matched her style.

Tim was blunter than a Ugandan aunt at a wedding

reception, and socially awkward at times, but he had a nice side too. He always sat next to Ace and greeted him in the morning with a new fact he'd learned about Uganda.

"Hey, 1962!" he yelled when Ace walked into the class.

"What?" Ace asked, staring at him.

"That's when Uganda gained independence from Great Britain, right? Cool. What's new with you?"

"I've been listening to some Kendrick Lamar. I'm also loving my English class, how about—"

Tim raised his finger to interrupt Ace. "You have the morning or afternoon class?"

"Afternoon, why?"

"Oh damn, you haven't heard then …"

"Heard what?" asked Ace.

"They're making us do group presentations starting next week on *To Kill a Mockingbird*. Working in groups can suck. I'm always doing all the work. It'd be better if we could pick our own team," Tim said glumly.

"Cool, cool …" Ace was about to ask another question when Tim placed his headphones over his ears. That was Ace's cue that Tim had had enough of their usual small talk.

In French class, there was Matilda St. Louis, passionate about activism, with short, black, braided hair and striking, warm brown eyes. She had a perky, somewhat clumsy character. Matilda and her family had spent the first six years of her life in the port city of Mombasa, Kenya. As a result, she was familiar with East African foods, cultures, and slang.

It was easier speaking with Matilda because she made Ace feel comfortable talking about stuff happening in his home country, and other topics like the climate change effects threatening many in the African continent.

"Jambo, Ace!" Matilda jumped from her seat as soon as he walked through the classroom doors. "Did you hear what happened in Congo last night? Oh, you're gonna freak!"

"What happened?" asked Ace.

"I read the Ugandan military was sent in to control rebels. Is that normal?"

"Yeah, it kinda is. It's more frequent than you can imagine. What protest are you hitting up after school?" joked Ace.

"It's wild that you can just read my mind. There's an anti-animal-cruelty protest happening near City Hall. I'll head there for a bit. I can't stay too long. Mom wants us home before Dad gets back. You should come with me to the protest. It'll be so much fun!" urged Matilda.

In an ideal world, Ace would have said 'yes' in a heartbeat. He also recalled how anxious his mother got when either he or his sister stayed out later without letting her know. Besides, political protest to an African parent was akin to wasting your time. If the event did not relate to school or career skills, it was not worth bringing up.

"Maybe next time," Ace said politely, knowing it was a lie.

"One of these days, Ace. One of these days, we're going to get you advocating for something. Mark my words!" Matilda said, chuckling.

Besides being a friendly face, Matilda helped Ace with his French. She created a cheat sheet of who to stay away from. On top of that list was the name Jamie Bishop, with multiple exclamation marks.

"Why's Jamie on here?" Ace asked.

"The most popular boy in our grade. All the girls call him 'The Swedish Prince.' Rumour has it that he may or may not be related to the royal family. If you ask me, he's a wolf in sheep's clothing. He'll pretend to be your friend, but don't trust him, Ace. Don't let those sparkling blue eyes and well-trimmed hair trick you into believing he's interested in protesting animal cruelty, or trick you into coming to school on a Sunday. Just don't!" warned Matilda.

Finally, there was Irons, the Phys Ed coach — a bald and muscular man with hardly any eyebrows. Ace liked Coach Irons because he reminded him of his old soccer coaches in Kampala. They paid attention to the players, gave pep talks, were more down-to-earth than the regular teaching staff. Like a distracted Kampala coach, however, Coach Irons always seemed to mix up the conversations he had with this students.

"Ace, you're right about the Raptors, buddy! This is

our year. We're gonna take that championship. Give it to me straight, what do you think about tonight's game?" Coach Irons would ask. Sometimes Ace thought it was Irons being silly.

"Coach, you're doing it again. I don't watch basketball. You were talking to Jacob about the Raptors yesterday, and I was talking to you about the English Premiership!"

"Gotcha! Right, we're talking about soc — I mean football. You trying out for the team?" Coach Irons asked.

"Umm … I don't think so … My mom says I should focus on my books, but …"

The lunch bell sounded, and Coach Irons ordered the students out of the gym. A second sooner and Ace would have answered honestly. "Hell yeah!" he wanted to blurt out to Coach Irons, but he held himself back. The feeling of frustration and disappointment loomed over him as he headed to the change room. He needed to clear his head and the sadness in his heart. He needed his peaceful place. The one location he felt safe to speak with the only person, he knew, would understand what he was going through: Olive.

At the top of the highest floor in one of the loneliest hallways, they met at the same time. Today, however, Olive just sat there with a blank face, like she'd seen a ghost. Her hands were not holding a lunch box but a graded test instead. In the top right hand corner, in a large bold red circle was the letter F.

"Oli, what's up?" Ace started.

"Do you miss it?" she replied.

"Miss what, exactly? Summer? Of course. Uncle Jackson taking us to the movies, seeing fireworks on Canada Day, walking around in shorts. You bet I miss the summer!" said Ace, trying to act coy, as if he did not see the failing grade scribbled on Olive's test.

"No, you idiot. Do you miss home? I miss it. I miss so much. I miss that everyone remembers you, even if they've just met you once. I miss my teachers making an effort to remind you that you are great and that we can accomplish anything."

Olive wrapped her arms around her legs and started to cry. Ace rushed to her side. Olive was the strong one. Even after their dad passed away a few years ago, it was Olive that held everyone together. She was their family's impenetrable wall. And now this wall was beginning to crack under cold Canadian conditions.

"What's wrong, sis?"

"Ace, I … I'm failing. I'm failing all my classes. I just failed a biology test. Biology, Ace! That's my thing! I was top of my class in Kampala, and I'm failing!"

Olive grabbed some tissues from her backpack to blow her nose.

"Did you study before the test, or …"

"Study? How and when do I have time? Mom's been busy, and I've been helping out with the chores and cooking. By the time everything is done, I'm way too tired. *You're* not even doing *your share,* so I end up doing double the work. It's hard enough at home, but I have no friends here. I'm trying everything to make myself sound *Canadian* but I can't … I just don't fit in well. I feel constantly judged and self-conscious about how I sound, dress, how I talk … Some of the girls said I'm a nerd for liking science. They don't even know there are teenage girls where we're from that would die to have this chance. I wanted to say that, but I didn't. So I try not to act smart to fit, and get an F. Now they don't want to partner with me for one of the projects. I just can't win. I can't, Ace …"

"I hear you, sis. I miss home, too. To be real, I've been feeling the same way since we got here. I wanted to talk to you about it, but also didn't want to bother you. I'm sorry I haven't been helping out at home. I can do better, and will, starting today." Ace reached out for his sister's hand.

"Thanks. We shouldn't keep things from each other. We've been through a lot since Dad died and coming to Canada."

Olive made a fist and released her pinky finger while signalling to Ace.

"Let's make a pact. We promise to tell each other everything and help each other out at home. Mom is going through a lot, so we need to be there for one another. Deal?"

"I've got your back and you got mine. Deal!" Ace

shook on their newest pledge. "What are you going to do about the test?"

"My teacher told me there's an after-school coaching program for students. I'm going to sign up, but I'll tell Mom first," Olive said, sounding earnest.

"You sure about that? She'll be pissed!"

"It's either I come clean or risk her finding out during a parent-teacher meeting," Olive replied. "She'll be furious at first, but if she knows I'll be doing coaching after school, I think that'll get her to calm down."

"So … In case she kicks you out for getting an F, can I get your room?" asked Ace slyly.

"You're such a villager!" Olive exclaimed, gently punching her brother before taking him into a hug.

CHAPTER 4
FROZEN

The greatest liar is the man who says he never lies.

– African proverb

English class always followed lunch. Besides sports and social studies, English had always been Ace's favourite growing up. He loved the feeling of opening up a brand-new book and exploring an author's strange new world and outlook on life. His father, when still alive, would always tell people: Ace learned how to read before he learned how to crawl and run.

The days got darker and the temperatures continued to drop. Without a video game console to keep him busy, Ace lost himself in the adventure books he borrowed from the Toronto Public Library. He was also beginning to appreciate some of the books recommended as part of his course work.

Grade 8 English was taught by Ms. Menon, a seasoned teacher who held herself in high regard and dressed like it too. From top to bottom, Ms. Menon looked like a lecturer at a prestigious private school with her signature pearl necklace. She was known for her strict nature and demand for excellence.

Ace felt a sense of familiarity and kinship with Ms. Menon. Not only was she aware of where Uganda was located on a map, but she also used her lessons to get the students to think outside the box and connect what they read with what was happening in real life. She was also one of the few teachers of colour at the school, and Ace felt comfortable asking her for help. That was, until after the Thanksgiving long weekend.

Ms. Menon began her class like she did normally with a call to order.

"People, people! Please sit down. We have three new students that have switched from the morning class to our afternoon class. I'm sure you are already acquainted by now. Given the change, I'll be switching up the working groups for the upcoming assignment." Ms. Menon stopped briefly when she saw a student raise their hand.

"Sorry, did you just say we have an assignment? Already? We just got here!" exclaimed Jamie Bishop while smirking at a few girls giggling right in front of him.

"Jamie Bishop, I presume. Your teachers ... have had a lot to say. I don't see why we all stop what we are doing just because you happened to join our class. This assignment will be due in two weeks, at the start of November. You should have ample time to work with your group members," Ms. Menon concluded, sternly.

"I can't work alone?" Jamie blurted out. "No offence to anybody, but group work slows me down. I can get a lot finished by myself."

"Mr. Bishop, this assignment is meant to help you and everyone. I'd suggest you get into your groups. I'll fill you in on what it actually entails, okay?" Ms. Menon's eyes widened on expressing the command.

Every student (with exception of Jamie) rose up to see the new groupings listed on the whiteboard behind Ms. Menon's desk. When Ace located his name, he was too stunned to speak. He'd been placed in Group D with his grade's most popular kids: Jamie Bishop, queen bee Becky Quinton, and Jamal Adelusi, the basketball savant.

This is it, Ace thought. *If this works out, everyone's going to know me. I just have to play it cool. Act cool, Ace. Act cool, fam.* He recalled all the famous high school movies he'd watched on TV and how being part of the cool group, or even simply being known to them, changed the destiny of the main character.

"Hey, Africa!" someone from the back shouted at Ace. It was Jamie waving him over to sit while Becky and Jamal snickered.

"Oh! Uh, for sure, fam!" Ace stammered, trying to find the right words. He moved his body as quickly as he could to sit down with his group mates. They all stared at him curiously without saying anything, until Jamie broke the silence.

"You're in my Art class, right?" Jamie asked.

"Jamie, you were just talking to me in Art class the other day," Ace replied.

"Oh, my bad, fam. Take it easy. I'm in a lot of classes and I talk to everyone. I'm really bad with names and faces too. Your name is …"

"It's Ace. Just Ace."

"Is that short for something? Do you have, like, a real 'African' name?" Jamie raised his fingers in air quotes.

"Bro, that ain't right," chided Jamal. "What do you mean by *real* African name? His name is Ace, leave it. What's up, little man?" Jamal fist-bumped Ace with a wink as if to say, *I got your back, brother.*

"Gosh, Jamie, quit being a douche for once. You're going to, like, give him the wrong impression. My name is Rebecca, but everyone calls me Becky, except for my mom. Glad to have you on our team. I heard you're pretty smart."

Becky was skinny, raven-haired, wore large round earrings and enough make-up to last for days. Her smile, however, made Ace lose all sense of self. He liked her.

"Attention, class!" Ms. Menon's voice snapped Ace back to reality. "For this group assignment, we'll all be reading *To Kill a Mockingbird* by Harper Lee. Each group will be assigned different chapters to present.

Every group member will provide a short presentation of the chapter they read and include references to plot, character, and literary devices used. Presentations will begin the first week of November, and leading us will be Jamie Bishop's group, Group D. Good luck everyone."

"Whatever!" said Jamie, rolling his eyes and brushing his hair aside. "This is a boring assignment anyway. I'll get my dad to hire some rando international student to do the assignment for me. Look at all those dweebs running up to ask for help!"

"I know, right," said Becky. "I get a bad vibe just looking at them. Losers, let me tell you. We're not losers, right, Ace? We're going to ace this assignment. See what I did there?" Becky giggled, and even though it sounded like a hyena crying, Ace couldn't stop admiring her perfect white teeth.

"Yeah, our man Ace got it. I got basketball tryouts, and I don't have time for this stuff. Ace, help a brother out, will ya?" Jamal asked.

"For sure, fam. I got ya'll. No sweat," Ace said, lying. This was the first group presentation he'd done in his school life. To make matters worse, he was terrified of speaking in front of crowds.

"We're countin' on ya, Africa," Jamie said with a grin.

Ace got an eerie feeling in his gut whenever he spoke with Jamie. Shivers coursed along his spine ... He couldn't place it, but something didn't feel right.

* * *

For days following the assignment announcement, Ace
did nothing but read and reread his group's assigned
chapters. He was such a regular at the school library that
the librarian remembered his name. Even during some
of his other classes, he'd sneak in a chapter and jot down
some notes. It had also become a problem at home when
Ace would forget to do his assigned chores after dinner.

Whenever his mother complained, Ace would say, "I
have a big assignment for school, Mom. I promise, I'll
get to it tomorrow." Which, of course, was a lie.

The assignment was all-consuming. But that was what
Ace may have needed. Another way he could escape
the reality of being homesick and not having friends
to share things with. On one occasion, he started to
daydream about the past. The one place he could once
again hear and see his late father, Godfrey, and his best
friends, Rodney and Ronan.

On a sunny afternoon day, Ace, Rodney, and Ronan
found themselves doing handstands against a concrete
wall overlooking Ace's front lawn. Supervising the
young boys was Ace's father, Godfrey Katumba. He was
seated on a plastic chair, book in one hand and a glass
of orange juice in the other.

Godfrey, as Ace remembered him before the cancer: a
bushy-browed, broad-shouldered man whose beard hid

a mischievous smile. His laugh infectious and gifted with a boastful voice that rang through the corridors.

"One more minute, gents! I got another funny one for you. How does the moon cut its hair?" Godfrey asked.

Ace sighed. "Oh brother, Dad finally has an audience for his lame jokes."

"Mr. Katumba, why are we practicing handstands when they have nothing to do with our school play?" asked Ronan briskly, trying not to lose his concentration.

"Don't be silly, Ronan," said Rodney. "Mr. Katumba is training our minds. Before we know it, we'll be moving things with our minds. I can already feel something … I don't think I can hold on!" Rodney fell on his stomach, followed by Ronan and Ace, who fell in a huge thud.

"I think what you're feeling, Rodney, is your foolishness increasing," said Ronan, picking himself off the ground.

"If I weren't dizzy and Mr. Katumba wasn't here, I would be prepared to dropkick you, Ronan. Just you wait! Mr. Katumba, did you see me?" asked Rodney as he staggered to his feet. Godfrey rushed over to get the boys to sit down.

"Rodney, we all saw you. Just take it easy. You just might move too much with your mind. You boys almost made two minutes and survived my dad jokes, too!" Godfrey chuckled.

"What was the point of that, Dad?" Ace asked, annoyed.

"You three gents have been using your entire weekend to practice for this school play. I love the dedication, but you also need to let your minds rest a little. Make room for some fun. It'll help with the nerves. I'm talking to you, Ace!" Godfrey pointed at his son. "You're all in this together."

"What if we mess up our parts, Dad? What if the other kids start laughing? We're acting in front of the whole school!" Ace cried.

"What if Rodney reads Ace's lines by mistake, or makes up his own?" asked Ronan.

"Ms. Tessa said I have talent and even remind her of a Hollywood star!" replied Rodney with an air of pride.

"Oh really? You sure she doesn't just say that to everyone with stuff to say in the play?"

"At least some of us have lines to say and aren't just trees in the background! Don't hate the player, Ronan, hate the game." Rodney winked before jumping behind Godfrey for protection.

"Calm down, everyone!" Godfrey insisted. "No one is going to mess up. Why don't you fear messing up when playing football in front of everyone?"

"There are people cheering for us when we play football, Dad. I feel energized, which helps me focus on the ball and communicate with my team when we're on the field," Ace explained.

"Exactly! You boys just need to think of acting in front of everyone like you're playing football. Imagine

I'm there, all your family members, too. All there, rooting for you. Focus on your lines like you would kick a football and just score. There's nothing to fear because you're all there to see each other win, right!"

"Right!" the boys replied in unison.

"Let's play a game of football before your mom gets back and sees I haven't started on dinner. But first … How does a moon cut its hair? Eclipse it! Get it? E-clips-it!" Godfrey burst out laughing.

"Where does your dad get his jokes?" Ronan asked Ace.

"Don't get me started, man. Don't get me started …"

Ace's mind brought him back to the present. Back in his basement apartment in cold Toronto. *What would Dad say,* Ace thought.

The answer came to him immediately: Ace needed to seek help from the one group of people at school he knew he could trust.

* * *

A week before presentation day, Ace arrived early to school on a Monday and waited nervously for the first period Art class.

King, Trivia, and Tower all strolled in together, laughing and cracking jokes. Trivia was first to notice something was up with Ace.

"What's cooking, Ace? Are you feeling the

49

gravitational pull from the full moon? I too have been unable to sleep soundly."

"No one cares about the damn moon, Trivia. Why don't you sign up with the NASA space club, or whatever they're called?" Dwayne jumped in.

"Eww, no. I'd rather join the debate team before the space club. Have you seen their club uniform? It's a crime that deserves to be reported to the fashion police!" exclaimed Trivia, throwing his hands up in disbelief.

"Everything okay, Ace? You seem shook," Tower asked, putting down his backpack. The trio of boys stared at Ace, noticing his burden.

Ace decided he could trust them with what he was feeling. He told them everything about English class, Group D with Jamie, Becky, and Jamal, as well as his fear of public speaking.

"Bro," said King, "I think I know what you're going through, because I get nervous before a big presentation, too."

"I get so sweaty that I bring two sets of shirts, just in case! Did you know that sweat is unique to everyone? It's like a fingerprint. I bet none of y'all knew that!" Trivia patted himself on the back.

"Don't mind him, man. I have something to share with you, Ace," Tower said. "So, last week I was partnered with some guy called Howard in my science class for an assignment. He seemed okay when we first met in class, but it all went downhill soon afterward. He never returned any of my texts or IG messages. He kept posting about hockey practice and his girlfriend, though.

"Anyway, he barely wanted to talk in class. When I reminded him the assignment was almost due, he brushed me off, saying he'd get his part done."

"What did you end up doing?" asked Ace.

"I spoke to King and Trivia about it. They told me I was being too nice about the whole thing. King joked that I should have unleashed my inner warrior and told them how I really felt. But for real, though, these guys pushed me to tell the teacher about it. It's a group project, after all, and everyone's supposed to pitch in. As nervous as I was, I told the teacher. She thanked me for the honesty and said that the assignment would be graded to reflect work effort. Howard failed the assignment and blocked me on his IG. He's a nothingburger anyway. I know it's hard, but you may have to speak with Ms. Menon."

"I don't know, bro," said Ace. "Jamal has tryouts, and I don't want to let him down. Becky ... Well, Becky has been really nice to me, and she keeps calling me smart. I don't want her to think I can't do it. And ... I'm afraid Jamie will think I'm a loser for asking for help," Ace confessed.

"Forget Jamie, man," said King. "Hold up. How about you send them a group message and tell them the truth, that they need to do their part? If they don't know you're struggling, then they can't help you. If they're cool as you say they are, they'll understand."

"S—sure ... I'll do that," Ace said anxiously, knowing he'd have to deliver some bad news to the cool kids.

"You're not alone, Ace. I know King listens to techno before a presentation, I do breathing exercises, and Tower practices in front of a mirror. I'll give you our numbers if you need to talk," said Trivia, handing over his phone for Ace to see the phone numbers of the trio.

"Trivia, why you gonna blast our business out like that?" said King. "I don't want people knowing what gets me hyped for a presentation."

"Maybe don't suggest a lame club for me to join and pick one that's fashion forward. Otherwise, I'll begin sharing more secrets. You feel me!" Trivia smirked.

"Ace, before I forget — Trivia, Tower, and I have started playing soccer at Regent Park after school. We couldn't make the team, but that don't mean we can't play some ball. We're calling it the Misfits league. Come join us!" King exclaimed.

"I'll think about it. Let me survive this assignment, and then we can talk," said Ace, acknowledging his friends' offer as the school bell rang, and the first class of the day began.

* * *

Right after his talk with his friends, Ace convinced Group D to create a WhatsApp group to chat about the assignment. It was there Ace decided to follow through on the Misfits' advice.

Ace: *Hi fam ☺, I was wondering if you guys can work on your own presentations for your chapters. I'm feeling a bit overwhelmed, and it's my first big presentation. I made some chapter notes to help y'all out after reading the whole book. Peace!*

Ace waited for the double blue checkmarks to reveal that everyone had read it. Jamie immediately responded.

Jamie: *☹ OMG, I'm so sorry to hear that you're overwhelmed, buddy. We should have known that this would be too much for one person. You're smart, but not that smart. Not to make this about me, but my dad has been feeling drained cause of his work, so we're out here skiing. Ace buddy, I don't want to stress my dad out by telling him I have schoolwork. Could you message me your notes on my chapter that I can use?*

Becky: *Ace, you're so sweet and lots of hugs ☺ Of course we'll help. You're like the smartest here. I have a Halloween party to plan this weekend ☹. Do you think you could at least help us with creating a top-notch presentation? XOXO*

Jamal: *It's all good bro, I can do my presentation if you help me out with my chapter. I read some of it before basketball practice*

Jamal's response made Ace feel a little bit better.

Ace: *I'm really sorry, guys. I'm sorry I let you down. I'm just a bit nervous about presenting and don't want to mess it up for anyone*

Jamie: *Don't sweat it bro. We got ya. You probably don't get to do these kinds of presentations in Kenya, right? How about you check out a YouTube video of the book and copy the script. It's so easy. I'm sure everyone is doing it. Who has time to read when there's way better things to do*

Ace: *Isn't that cheating tho??*

Jamie: *It's not cheating if it's publicly available information. Besides, we do it all the time and the teachers won't do jack. Trust me!* ☺

* * *

Presentation day had arrived. Ace had spent the entire

morning and lunch preparing his lines and notes from his assigned chapter. He'd wished everyone good luck in the Group D message group, but only Jamal responded with *Good luck, bro!*

When English began, Ms. Menon had rearranged the class chairs to make extra space for the presenting team to showcase their work. After calling the class to attention, she asked for Group D to come up and present.

"Group D, who'll be kicking us off with a Chapter One review?" Ms. Menon asked.

"I believe that will be Ace, Ms. Menon. We'll present our parts afterward. Ace just couldn't wait for this presentation," Jamie mocked, laughing with Becky in matching black and white sweater vests.

"Ace, take it away!" said Ms. Menon.

Ace could feel the sweat from his palms and his heart beating at an increased rate. He held out his sheets of paper with notes and briefly looked at the class. Something was wrong. His mind was reading, but the words failed to come out of his mouth. It was if he'd had a spell cast on him, which stopped him from moving or speaking. He was so petrified of being in front of everyone that he froze still for several minutes.

"Ace? Ace, is everything okay?" Ms. Menon rose from her seat. She walked slowly to him as the rest of the class sat there in silence. Jamie Bishop got out his phone to record the entire situation.

Ms. Menon patted Ace's shoulder. "It's okay, Ace. You got yourself some stage fright. How about you sit down and the other members present their parts. We can talk after class. Does that sound okay to you?"

Ace could only remember nodding his head and agreeing to whatever was said. The sheer embarrassment stopped him from looking at anyone or anywhere other than the whiteboard overlooking the classroom.

Even when the final home bell rang, Ace was glued to his seat until everyone left and only Ms. Menon was left in the classroom. He could overhear Jamie exclaiming in the hallway, "Did you guys just see Mr. Freeze in real life? Who knew he was from Africa!"

Ms. Menon tried to comfort Ace, but he was awash in tears, feeling overwhelmed and ashamed.

"Ace, it's okay. Everyone's gone now. Do you want to talk?" Ms. Menon asked softly.

"I ... I ... I'm sorry. I failed everyone. I thought ..." he mumbled.

"It's perfectly normal to feel what you are feeling, Ace. It was bit scary for you. We can work on that together for next time. You shouldn't feel ashamed. I've been there," Ms. Menon explained.

"You ... have?" Ace said, surprised.

"Oh, more times than I can remember. It gets better and easier. We can work on it, okay? You just tell me what you need."

Ace timidly asked, "Can I sit here for a bit longer? Is that okay with you?"

"If that's what you need, I'll give you the space. I'm just going to be sitting over by my desk. You can let me know when you're ready to go. I'll be right here with you." Ms. Menon quietly walked away.

"Thank you, Ms. Menon," Ace said, wiping tears from his face.

CHAPTER 5

LOST

A child that is encouraged grows up with confidence.
— Ugandan proverb

Once the hallways were clear enough and Jamie nowhere to be seen, Ace went straight to his locker on the first floor of the building. He grabbed his puffy yellow winter jacket, gloves, and toque, and raced out of the school building.

With tears dripping from his eyes, all Ace wanted at this very moment was to call a friend. But who? Olive was busy with her after-school program. Ace didn't want her worrying about him. She was also trying to do her best. Ronan and Rodney were too far to reach, and in a different time zone.

He had no other option than to walk home, head held down. Strolling along Dundas Street East, he thought of his father and what he'd say had he still been alive:

"Ace-Point! Don't ever let life get you down, my son. There will always be obstacles. Whenever life gets you down, tackle it head-on."

He imagined Olive beside him, saying, "Listen here, Villager, you are bigger than anything that comes before you."

Ace cried even more, knowing how disappointed his friends and family would have been knowing that he wasn't able to face his presentation head-on. The pain he felt slowly morphed to anger. Anger at his new world, and anger against his mother.

Why did Mom have to move us? Was it really worth it? Was it worth it to take us from our home and everything we know to place where we are nothing or less than that? I feel so lost!

All of a sudden, Ace heard a familiar voice: "Ace! Ace! Over here, fam! Come join us before it gets dark."

It was Dwayne the King waving eagerly, trying to get Ace's attention. He and the other two Misfits, Trivia and Tower, were playing in one of the open soccer fields near Regent Park. King took hold of the black-spotted soccer ball and kicked it in Ace's direction.

In that moment, an even deeper voice, something deep within Ace, made him drop everything and run toward the ball, commanding it to the ground. He flipped it from behind his foot and headed it toward the netless goal post.

"Sweet pepper!" Trivia exclaimed, astonished. "He wasn't kidding about his skills!"

"Bro, that was dope! The way you ran for the ball and did whatever you did. You should have tried out for the team," Tower said.

"Maybe you can show us a thing or two, bro. You're living up to your name, fam. By the way, how did it go?" King asked, meaning the English presentation.

"I … I … I'd rather not talk about it," Ace said hesitantly. "Could we just play some ball before it gets dark? I need this right now."

"Sure, fam. We don't need to talk about it. Let's just kick it. We finally got an African that can play ball. Trivia, it's time the big dogs show you how we play soccer!" King said.

"You think you're so good, eh, King! You can't handle the truth!" Trivia took hold of the ball. He attempted to shoot into the direction of Ace, King, and Tower, but it diverted and hit the window of a dark grey car speeding past.

The car came to a halt. It was not just any ordinary car. It was a Toronto Police cruiser driving through the neighbourhood. The car came to a halt, and two uniformed officers exited their automobile to approach the four boys.

"Damn it, Trivia! This is why your mom don't let you have Orange Crush right after 3:00 p.m. You have two left feet or something," King angrily remarked.

"One, it'd be impossible to have two left feet, and two, I can't help it that I'm strong and cute at the same time. It's a curse I have to live with," Trivia replied. Tower silently shook his head in disbelief.

As the officers moved closer to the boys, a pit grew in Ace's stomach. He knew they were in some sort of trouble.

"Dwayne, buddy!" said one of the moustached officers with beach sand hair. "You know better than to be playing so close to sunset. What if that ball smashed into someone else's car?"

"Ya, ya, I know. Fam, this is Matt. He volunteers at the community centre where my mom works. Matt, we just wanted to kick the ball around before heading back home."

"Kick the ball … How did the tryouts go?" Matt asked.

"We didn't make the team, man. At least we tried. I wish Ace over here signed up when we had a chance, though. He's dope," King replied.

Ace shook his entire body as if to deny the compliment being bestowed on him while trying to avoid the gaze of the officers. "No, no … I'm ordinary. Nothing special here. You know, I think it's time I head home, too."

"Dwayne, why don't you bring him to play some indoor soccer? It's not outdoors, but at least you get to kick the ball somewhere indoors in the fall. Think about it!" Matt suggested.

"Ya, sure … So we can go home now?"

"Excuse me, Officer!" exclaimed a voice behind Officer Matthew, a voice familiar only to Ace. "Why is my son being questioned by the police?"

"Oh, hello, ma'am. I'm Constable Matthew, and next to me is Constable O'Neil. The boys were playing a game of soccer when their ball bumped into our car. We just wanted to have a chat. Nothing to worry yourself with." Matthew smiled while confronted with Zzabu's poker face.

"He's not in trouble, is he? He can go home?" Zzabu asked, still worried.

"Of course! We were just about wrapped up here. Just telling the lads to come join in on some indoor soccer. I hear your boy is pretty good, based on rave reviews from his friends." Matthew winked, gesturing at King, Trivia, and Tower.

"O–okay … We'll think about it," said Zzabu as she yanked Ace away from his friends to rush back home, her face full of fear, worry, and shame.

CHAPTER 6

SACRIFICE

If a child eats sour fruit, it is the parent's teeth that are set on edge.

– African proverb

Ace didn't know what was worse: being caught getting questioned by a pair of police officers for the entire neighbourhood to see, or being scolded by his mom both in English and Luganda on the front steps of their home.

Suffice it to say, the mood over dinner that evening was uncomfortable, tense, and awkward.

No sooner had both Ace and Olive finished the last grain of rice on their plate than Zzabu finally allowed herself to speak. She'd been silent, even ignoring Olive's school updates and small talk about the changing weather.

"Your school called today, Ace," Zzabu said calmly. "Your teachers are concerned with your grades. Is there something you want to share? Are you in a gang, Ace? Are you doing drugs?"

"N–no, Mama. I'd never. Promise. I was just out playing with my friends after school and we kicked the ball by accident. We weren't thinking. We'd never do anything stupid," Ace tried to explain.

"You *definitely* were not thinking! Do you take yourself to be a Canadian now? Do you think you can do as you wish and go where it pleases you? What is going on, Ace? I did not bring you here to act a fool! Not only must I worry about your grades, but police, too? You've seen the news. What if something had gone wrong?"

All of Ace's emotions erupted. "You know what feels wrong? Being here! Why did you bring us here? Why did you take us from our home? Why did we have to leave everything behind?" Ace demanded.

"Because the choice wasn't ours, Ace," Zzabu said, her anger turning to sorrow. "The choice wasn't ours. Your father and I wanted the best for you, and Canada was there to help us in our moment of trouble. I'm trying my best to help get us settled, and I need you guys to do your part. Seeing you succeed gives me hope that everything hasn't been in vain. I'm too tired to continue with this now. You two clear up the dining table and the rest of the dishes in the sink. After I get back from my shower, Ace, I want to hear a plan on how these grades are going up!"

Zzabu got up from her chair and headed toward her room.

* * *

"How're you feeling, kiddo?" Olive asked.

"I feel terrible. I feel like a jerk for speaking to Mom that way. I've never seen her *that* upset before," Ace said.

"She's worried for us. You especially!" Olive pointed with her mouth.

"Why me?"

"Do you not watch the news, silly? There are so many stories of young Black girls and boys getting in trouble with the police. Stories of young Black men getting stabbed or shot at before they even reach graduation. She just doesn't want us to be another statistic or news article," Olive explained.

Ace shrugged. "I get that, but why was she so upset when I talked about home? Why did she say we didn't have a choice? I thought you told me she was starting a new job ... Was that a lie?"

"Listen, Mom was planning on telling you soon, but you deserve to know the truth about why we left Uganda. You know that Mom is a journalist, right?"

"I know that. What does that got to do with anything?"

"Everything! A few years ago, before Dad passed away, Mom wrote some news articles that exposed powerful business people misusing taxpayer money for illegal activities. Case closed, right? That's what Mom and Dad thought, too.

"Right around the time Dad was diagnosed with cancer, Mom started receiving death threats and people started showing up at her office. It got worse when a judge allowed for the release of the corrupt business people Mom helped put away. They swore revenge for the public humiliation."

"Why didn't I know about this? No one said anything!"

"Mom and Dad didn't want you to worry. They wanted you to enjoy being a kid. I only found out because Mom was depending on me more when Dad's cancer got worse. Then a charity in Canada called Journalists for Human Rights offered to help resettle our family with help from some UN refugee agency. To help with the costs, Mom and Dad had to sell everything, even the house. There was no turning back for us.

"Mom is still trying to find full-time work while working part-time for the Journalists for Human Rights. She might even need to return to school because some of her credentials aren't good enough. She's under a lot of stress," Olive said.

"I really didn't know, Olive. What do I do now?"

"Leave the job stuff with Mom. She'll make it work. Uncle Jackson is also helping out here and there. You and I just need to focus on our grades and make friends. Who are they, anyway? You know, I made friends, too. At my after-school program. Leticia and Halima," Olive said, smiling.

"Hmm … I thought this was about me and my friends, loser?" Ace laughed while splashing water from a nearby glass onto Olive.

"Brainless villager! You throw water like a starving goat. Here, I'll show you how women throw!"

Olive grabbed a full cup of water and began to chase Ace with it. They both enjoyed a few minutes of happiness before their mother yelled out, "I hope to see the dishes sparkling clean and the dining room table spotless when I'm out of this room!"

"Yes, Mama!" they yelled back in unison, heading back to the kitchen to finish off their chores as they chuckled at each other.

CHAPTER 7

OUTCASTS

A friend at hand is better than a far-distant relative.

— African proverb

Rrrriiinnnggg!

The lunch bell echoed throughout the school. While his classmates zoomed to the cafeteria as usual, Ace was on his way to a new spot, one that had been suggested to him by the Misfits.

The Art room was managed by Ms. Reid. King, Trivia, and Tower spoke the world of her. Others like Jamie had nothing but terrible things to say.

* * *

Days before the whole presentation snafu, Ace recalled Jamie and Becky talking about Ms. Reid.

"Take it from me, Africa," Jamie said, "you don't want

to be hanging around the Art room any time during or after lunch, especially with Ms. Reid there."

"Why?" asked Ace.

"Gosh, why?" Becky cut in. "She's the worst. My boyfriend's cousin knew a girl who said she was forced to watch a nature documentary about saving rainforests during the lunch period. She asked everyone to share what they're doing to help save the environment. It's called a lunch-time break, not a nerd fest. It gives me nightmares just thinking about it!"

"I heard she lets the nerds from Anime club take up the space on Fridays. Good luck trying to get your art project done before lunch. Take it from me, Africa, she's the Queen of Nerds. Just stay clear," Jamie advised.

Funnily, the Art room didn't sound so bad. Nature documentaries and anime during lunch sounded like heaven. The Canadian kids had it good with their teachers. They didn't have to face the humiliation of being publicly spanked with bamboo sticks by their teachers, in front of the entire school, like a scene from *The Hunger Games*.

* * *

Ace really didn't know what to expect other than what was in his imagination. To his surprise, it was way better. Some students were quietly working away on art projects with music playing. A few other students huddled together watching anime and dressed in colorful costumes, and all the others were just having their lunch while helping out in the art room. On a silvery steel stool supervising them all was Ms. Reid with her curly brown hair, green horn-rimmed glasses, and a welcoming smile.

"Ohhh … Hold your horses, people. I think we've got a new lunch joiner! Welcome, welcome! Good to see you back here, Ace! Those guys would *not* stop talking about you," said the woman cheerfully, pointing to the Misfits. The trio were rolling their eyes.

"Umm … thank you… Ms. … Katia Reid."

"Ace, Ms. Reid is just fine. Enjoy the fun and excitement of our Grade 8 creative lounge!" Ms. Reid flung her arms up in the air as if she'd finished some interpretive dance.

"Creative … lounge?" Ace asked in shock. "Isn't this just our classroom?"

"It is, fam," said King from the back of the room. "Don't get it twisted. Ms. Reid just likes to put polish on everything!"

"Dwayne is right, the Art room just sounds so dull and boring. I want some razzle dazzle. I just want you guys to have a safe space to do your homework, eat lunch, and talk about whatever is going on. This is totally your space … *Fam*!" Ms. Reid said with a wink.

"Ms. Reid, it sounds so weird when you say it. You gotta add some fire to it. You know what, leave it to us," King yelled.

"You know what, Dwayne? Seeing as you are in such a cooperative spirit, why don't you show Ace what you three are helping me with?"

"Come kick it, fam." King gestured to Ace.

"How did it go with your mom?" Trivia asked, looking sadder than usual. "I'm grounded for a week and can't have any Orange Crush for a month."

"Oh no, what are we to do? Will you be able to survive?" Tower mocked.

"You don't know the struggle! Good thing I stocked up on enough Orange Crush supply in my locker. Did you know that pop doesn't expire and it's good three months after its expiry date?" A mischievous smile grew on Trivia's face.

King raised his eyebrow. "You know you have a problem, right?"

"Just let me live my life, King! At least I don't listen to Céline Dion on my way to school," Trivia clapped back.

For whatever reason, Ace began to laugh out loud for everyone in the room to hear. He couldn't remember the last time he laughed so hard his stomach hurt. The last time it happened was probably during one of his misadventures with Rodney and Ronan.

"You okay, Ace?" Tower asked.

"Ha! Yeah! I am great, actually. You guys reminded me of my old friends, is all. I feel like myself around you guys, and you look out for me. You also know what it's like being an immigrant to Canada," Ace noted.

"Oh, I was born here, fam," King said. "My mom and dad are from Trinidad and Tobago. I get to go home once a year. But unlike some of our classmates, I can read a map."

"Say less! I've been in classes where some kids sweat when you ask them where Vietnam or Botswana are on a map." Trivia giggled.

"I know, right!" The words just jumped out of Ace's mouth.

"Isn't it weird that kids know almost all the cities in Europe, but they think Africa is a country?" Tower said, shaking his head.

"You see that too, right!" Ace exclaimed.

"Fam, we hear it all the time. That's how we all became friends. You wanna join our crew, Ace?" King asked.

Ace was speechless. After weeks of being alone, here he was finally being asked to join a crew. Not just any crew: people who saw and heard him for who he was.

"Yes! I mean … If you guys are cool with me joining, of course," Ace said, trying to contain his excitement.

"Cool. We meet here every lunch period. After school, we normally play some soccer outside, but since it's getting colder we'll be heading over to Tower's place to play video games. I think you told us already, but where are you from again?" King asked Ace.

"Uganda. I'm from Uganda," Ace said excitedly.

"Dwayne, Ace, Lutti, and Ericksen!" hollered Ms. Reid. "It's really wholesome to see a new friendship blossom, but you folks promised to help me out before the end of lunch. Can I get those brushes cleaned … fam?"

"Yes, Ms. Reid!" all four boys said in unison, laughing.

CHAPTER 8
TALENT

As long as you keep a green branch in your heart, you will always find a bird singing.

— South African proverb

It was a Saturday afternoon. The sky was as grey as gravel. The air was so tense, you could slice it with a knife. Ace treaded cautiously as his boots sank into the soft, cushy snow. He turned to his right to check on his partner, Trivia, who was looking around nervously while holding on tightly to a ball of snow in his gloved hand.

Toronto received an early dose of snow in November. Although it was to be short-lived, the Misfits could not waste an opportunity to have fun. Seeing and feeling the snow for a Ugandan who had only known sun and rain was like experiencing an undiscovered wonder of the world. If it were up to Ace, he'd spend the entire day outside rolling around in the fluffy particles to his heart's content. But he had a game to win.

"Take it easy, Trivia," Ace whispered. "You're breathing loud enough for the entire city and Mars to hear us coming. *Shhh*!"

"*Shhh* yourself, man! I told you I don't do well under stressful situations. I clam up, I breathe a lot, and I can't stop talking. Like, do you know that snow isn't white but translucent. It's actually–"

POW! POW!

Multiple snowballs knocked Trivia off his feet and to the ground.

"Ouch!" Trivia cried as King and Tower jumped out from a nearby shrub, throwing several snowballs in Ace and Trivia's direction.

Without any hesitation, Ace rolled to the ground like the action heroes he so admired. He threw his gloves aside and dug his freezing fingers deep into the snow. He shaped it quickly into a large enough sphere and tossed it like his life depended on it.

"I ain't going down without a fight!" Ace yelled, but he only heard King and Tower laughing wickedly.

POW! POW! POW! POW!

Ace felt the cold impact and onslaught of snowballs strike his face and body. He raised his arms to yield.

"Geez! We get it! You guys beat us!" Ace shouted.

"So what did ya think! Pretty dope way to enjoy your first day of snow, right?" King smirked in his black puffy winter jacket and black-and-gold Raptors cap.

"This was so much fun, bro! Where are we, though? I don't think I've been here before. We definitely don't have parks like this in Kampala." Ace admired the huge public park with an empty tennis court gathering snow, dog park valley, several large trees with naked branches, and a variety of food and coffee shops across the street.

"Trinity Bellwoods, fam. It was Tower's idea," King said.

"We got ya! We saw you blow up the chat group with pictures of snow, and we knew we had to treat our boy right," said Tower.

"There's nothing childish about making snow angels! You're all Neanderthals for thinking that way. By the way, creative people live longer!" exclaimed Trivia as he picked himself off the ground.

"Where to next?" Ace asked eagerly. The other boys looked at each other and smiled back at Ace.

"Have you tried poutine yet?" asked King.

Just like that, Ace knew he was in for an adventure with his new friends.

* * *

The end of November had become a bright light for Ace. While some students loathed the idea of lunch in the Art room (or creative lounge, as Ms. Reid put it), this was Ace's favourite hour of the day. He got to leave the stress of home life and school life aside and hang with his buddies. As the days flew by, their friendship grew.

Their meet-ups were no longer confined to lunch. The gang of misfits, as Trivia referred to them, met every morning before the first school bell, at lunch period in the school cafeteria, and of course after school.

It wasn't long before their hangouts extended into the weekend. The one rule: Ace had to be home by six in the evening. Even though his mom had moved past the Regent Park incident, Ace had a curfew to follow until his grades improved.

In spite of that, the Misfits always found a way to work within their restrictions. They even set up a TikTok group to post a new video of themselves each day trying something new. Learning how to ice skate with both Ace and Trivia constantly falling flat on their faces. Trying a Vietnamese dish called pho in Kensington Market. Waiting in line for some Jamaican beef patties. Trivia tricking Ace into believing Beaver Tails were made from actual beavers' tails. Dancing with performers by Yonge and Dundas Square. And the snowball fight on the first day of snow. Ace's loneliness had slowly started to fade away, and a new feeling emerged: hope.

* * *

It was the first day of December, and the Misfits decided to convene in the Art room for lunch.

"Did you see it? Did you all see it?" Trivia came rushing through the Art room doors, even forgetting to greet Ms. Reid.

"Take a chill pill, Trivia! What's got you so hyped, fam? Your mom forgot to pack your lunch again?" King joked.

"King! I'm being serious. The New Year talent show. The school is opening it up to Grades 8 and 9 this year! This is my time to shine as an actor. This could be my origin story. I can see the headlines now: *South African prince dazzles school crowd in Oscar-worthy performance!*" Trivia said in his usual dramatic way.

"There's being real, and then there's delusional. Which one are you, Trivia?" Tower asked. He rolled his eyes as he bit into his sandwich.

"You jest, good sir, but I'll have you know that I was given five gold stars for my Grade 5 performance of *Jack and the Beanstalk*. It moved many to tears. The crowd gave thunderous applause," Trivia insisted.

"Did they clap because it was over or because they took pity on you? There's a difference," King remarked.

Then King's face lit up. "Yo! I have an idea. How about we do something … together, like as a team?"

"What!" Ace jumped. "No, no, no … I don't think that would be a good idea, guys. I don't do well with crowds. Not anymore."

"I am of course offended by King's comments, but he couldn't recognize talent even if it slapped him in the face," said Trivia. "But, Ace, you don't strike me as the shy type. You never shut up about how you led your primary school soccer team to victory. What changed?"

"I ... I ... don't want to talk about it."

"Bro, we don't hide stuff here. What's wrong?" Tower insisted.

"Fine ... You remember the day I found you guys at Regent Park? Well ... The reason I was there in the first place was because I messed up on my English presentation." Ace noticed his heart racing just recalling the events.

"Was it because you took a look at King's ugly mug and couldn't stomach the horror?" Trivia joked.

"Not now, Trivia ... We weren't even near that class. Let Ace finish," King said.

"I froze up ... I just stood there and did nothing ... Because I was afraid. My sister calls it stage fright. It was so humiliating. I felt so dumb. This always happens to me. I stood there for five minutes like a zombie. I failed my group, and I looked like a loser. That's why I can't do it. I can't do the talent show. You're better off finding someone else," Ace said.

For the first time, Ace was relieved to hear the end of lunch bell. He could run from this uncomfortable situation without the others throwing their pity at him.

"Sorry, guys, I have English class. We have a quiz today, and I should get going. Catch you guys later," said Ace as he quickly packed up and left the Art room. The rest of the Misfits were still stunned by what they had heard.

CHAPTER 9

OTHERING

The only thing to do with good advice is to pass it on.
— Ugandan proverb

Ace was in his last class of the day when he felt the phone in his pocket vibrate. It was a text from King.

Bro, it's messed what happened. Catch you outside after school. Gotta tell ya something. Be easy!

"Say less," Ace responded as he wondered what his friend had to share.

By the front steps of the school, Ace waited patiently for his friends to show. To his surprise, it was only King that came flying out the large doors.

"Where's Trivia and Tower?" Ace asked.

"They just left through the back," King said casually.

"What the hell, King? You could have at least told me.

I've been waiting here for you guys," Ace said angrily.

"Relax, fam. It's just me and you today. We gotta talk about what you told us at lunch." King had them start walking on Queen Street East.

"I don't wanna talk about it, King. Let it go."

"Why're you being a punk, Ace?"

"What'd you say? Say it again!" Ace pushed up against him.

"You heard me. Why're you being a punk? We're your friends, Ace. We got your back. Why you actin' like a punk? You acting like you're the only one that's messed up. You think you're the only one who's been messed with by Jamie Bishop. The world doesn't revolve around you. If you hadn't run like a punk after lunch, I'd have told you that it happened to me, too!"

"King ... I didn't know."

"You never asked me. You never tell us anything but the good stuff. You know my parents are separated and I have to split my time at two different homes every week. You know Tower's grandma was just diagnosed with cancer. You know Trivia has ADHD and has problems focusing in class. You know this because we share. We're friends!

"Back in grade school, when I found out my parents were separating, I was crushed. I didn't have a lot of friends then and stammered a lot. I didn't know how to talk about it with anyone. All the other kids kept talking about their family trips and traditions while mine was breaking apart. There was one kid that knew what I was going through, and that was Jamie Bishop.

"I don't know how he saw me, but he came up to me after class one day and said I looked sad. I hate lying, so I told him the truth. He told me his parents had been divorced for a few years. He said it sucked, but he didn't have to hear them yell at each other anymore. They kept trying to buy his love after the separation. He told me he got my back. I believed him.

"In Grade 7, we had to do some project on our family tree. I didn't want to do it, but the teacher told me if I didn't she'd rat me out to my parents. She was a punk. Anyway, I presented my family tree but didn't say anything about the separation. Jamie had his own plans. He put up his hand and asked whether my parents were still together and if I had any siblings in Trinidad I didn't know about. To add to it all, he asked if my parents were even married. The whole class couldn't stop laughing, and I was just there, frozen and ashamed. I was mad, embarrassed to have shared something personal that Jamie used against me.

"Funnily enough, before the teacher ordered the class to stop, it was Trivia, a new kid then, who stood up to Jamie by splashing half a bottle of Orange Crush on his face and calling him out. 'Ya think every dad is like yours, Jamie?' Jamie was about to lace him when he was blocked and pushed to the ground by our boy Tower. Why you think Jamie doesn't mess with us? He's terrified of Trivia and Tower. He hates being reminded of that day, when someone was willing to stand up to a bully like him.

"Ever since then, Trivia and Tower are my boys for life. Even if they can't dance. Ace, you have to believe me when I say that we got ya back!"

There was a moment of pause before Ace said his next words. King spoke from the heart. He was real and genuine. He shared with Ace as his old friends Rodney and Ronan did many times over. He knew and believed, without a doubt, that King, Trivia, and Tower would be there for him.

"Wow ... Well, thanks, man. In my family we have a saying ... We don't run away from our problems but face them head-on. I guess a part of me still thought you guys wouldn't understand. But I was wrong, fam." Ace fist-bumped King.

"Cool. So we're entering this contest, then? Ace, I believe in you. You gotta do it, man. You're called Ace for a reason. You're the number one guy that gets stuff done. You're also the smartest guy I know, even smarter than Trivia. You want to conquer that stage fright of yours, let your voice be heard. Rise up, brother, we have a contest to win!"

"Hmm ... All right ... I'm in!" Ace said with a

smile, feeling relieved and supported. "But there's still something I need to share with you and the fam. I need to tell you the full story of why we came to Canada."

CHAPTER 10
DIFFERENT IS COOL

The eyes of our elders do not shed tears for no reason.
— Ugandan proverb

Of the seasons Ace had seen and experienced, none was more joyful than Christmas. The neighbourhood houses were decked out in warm, coloured lights, large and well decorated Christmas trees, different variations of inflatable Santa Claus riding his sleigh. And then there were the shopping malls and cafés that served up festive drinks and desserts while continuously playing "All I Want for Christmas" by Mariah Carey.

Uncle Jackson, who normally seemed indifferent to festivities, was in an unusually joyful state each evening when he stopped by to help Ace with his homework. He wore a different red Christmas sweater and greeted everyone with a new Christmas-themed song. Even Ace's mom came alive when she heard his signature knock on the door.

This would be Ace's first Christmas in Canada with his family. Like many things this year, it did not feel quite the same. He was used to celebrating the holiday in sunny, warm weather and among his closest relatives. Gift buying was not as much of a thing in Kampala. You were more likely to get a kid's novel than an Xbox. The best kind of gift was a shared meal, games, and dancing to the latest hits.

Canadians were a lot more giving during this time of the year. Ace's teachers would bring treats to school and ask about their students' holiday plans. Even Olive and her friends had organized a cupcake and samosa holiday sale to fundraise for local refugee families from the Democratic Republic of Congo. They'd raised over $2,000 for the family.

Before classes broke off for Christmas break, King surprised everyone with personally designed t-shirts and bracelets that read "*#MisfitSquad*." For Ace, this was another sign that he had finally found his people and friends.

"Here's the plan," King began. "It's going to be family time over the next couple of days. My grandma won't let me out of her sight. But we gotta start thinking of how we're gonna crash it at that talent show this January. Any ideas?"

"I got an idea," Ace said confidently. "We should do a speech."

"A speech?" Trivia groaned. "Brother, what expired almond milk did you have this morning? How is a speech supposed to showcase my skill as an *actor*?"

Tower raised his hand. "I'm not a speech guy, but I can design the visuals."

"No, we won't give the speech. *Ace* will." King nodded at Ace.

"Okay, is there something in the water? Did I mysteriously end up in an alternative dimension? Is Beyoncé still not the queen? What is happening?" Trivia sounded bemused.

"Trivia, the only way Ace is going to get over his stage fright is by facing his fear, not running from it. You did it for me, so let's do it for our boy. Tower is going to work on the visuals, I'll work on the music, and Trivia, you'll be working on the trivia facts for the speech," King explained.

"Wait up, wait up! What's the speech going to be about, Ace?" Trivia asked.

"You know how the school likes to say it's accepting of people like us that are different and diverse? I wanna talk about that ... That it's cool to be different. It's cool to have friends that think different and are different because that's how we grow. By learning from each other. And in turn, that's how we become better to each other. So, like, different is cool," said Ace.

"Wow, that's deep!" said Tower.

"You may have caught my curiosity," said Trivia. "I want to hear more."

"We have an idea now," said King. "Ace, my man, use the holiday time to come up with some words to inspire. We'll start working on our parts. I bet we can get Ms. Reid to help us out with some props. Let get it!"

* * *

When school resumed following the holiday break, the Misfits regrouped every day after school to work on their project in the Art room. Ms. Reid, after much urging from King, decided to lend the squad a hand with designing some playful props for Ace's big speech, alongside Tower's visuals. King had started compiling some music to help set the stage. Trivia had the responsibility of running through Ace's speech and fact-checking every detail and statistic. Everything seemed to be going as planned.

One lunch period, King convinced the squad to meet in the gymnasium instead.

"We've been working day and night on this speech. Let's take it easy today. A change of scenery is good for everyone."

The Misfits found some benches to sit on, enjoy their lunch, and watch whatever sport Coach Irons had allowed. To Ace's surprise, the coach had organized drop-in indoor soccer. The students seemed to have divided themselves into two groups for the activity — red shirts and blue shirts. Ace saw Jamie playing on the blue shirts team, which was already winning by three goals to zero.

"Ace!" Trivia exclaimed. "Get in there and give the red shirts a hand. You keep telling us about your soccer days. Show us."

"Nah, I'll sit this one out. I can play next time," Ace lied. Every cell in his body just wanted to jump onto the gym floor, but he could hear the voice of doubt whispering, *You're a joke. You couldn't even handle a short presentation and now you think you can dribble a ball and win against Jamie? Just do what you do and sit this one out.*

"Too scared to play, Africa?" mocked Jamie. "Afraid you'll freeze up again like in English class?" Jamie pretended to faint.

Tower stood up and walked over to the basket next to Coach Irons. He grabbed a red pinnie and threw it at Ace.

"Get in there and make him eat his words!"

The self-doubt was drowned out by Tower's command. It was as if Ace's body went on autopilot. He saw himself pick up and put on the red pinnie, then raced onto the court. In mere seconds, he managed to whisk the ball away from a striker in blue. He dribbled through not one but four defenders and finally scored the red team's first goal. The gym roared.

When the blue team, led by Jamie, tried attacking again, Ace managed to steal the ball and dribble around him, but not before Jamie tripped over his own feet and fell. Ace got through the defence again and scored a second goal. The spectators, especially the Misfits, cheered again.

Jamie turned red on hearing the crowd cheer for Ace. He got angrier after Ace passed the ball through Jamie's legs to score another goal, which caused the crowd to laugh. One of Jamie's teammates pointed at him while making chicken gestures with his arms. "Bro, that kid made you lay an egg to win!" In a matter of seconds, the entire gymnasium, with exception of Coach Irons, who was trying his best to hide his amusement, began making chicken sounds and chanting, "Jamie laid an egg! Jamie laid an egg!"

"Go kick rocks!" Jamie yelled, throwing down his blue pinnie.

"It's just a game, bro. You sure you're not the one that froze up today?" Ace winked at him.

"You think you're some baller after the cheap stunts you pulled today. You're nothin', Africa. I'm gonna make you pay for making a fool out of me. Watch yourself!" Jamie warned.

"Oh, what, you gonna lay some more eggs for us?" said King in between laughs, which further enraged Jamie.

Jamie went to grab one of the indoor soccer balls and

kicked it in the direction of the Misfits. It missed Trivia's head by a few hairs. Furious, Ace rushed to Jamie and pushed him to the floor. Fighting back, Jamie rose to his feet, closed his knuckles, and swung his left arm across Ace's jaw.

CHAPTER 11

UNITY

One finger cannot extract thorns from a foot.

— Ugandan proverb

News of the altercation found its way to Ace's mother that evening.

"Fighting! So you're a fighter now!" Zzabu said in disbelief. "What am I going to do with you, Ace? You're getting in trouble with the police and now you're picking fights in school. What is going on, my son?"

"It's not what you think, Mama," Ace tried to explain. "We were playing a friendly game of soccer when one of the boys kicked the ball at my friends on purpose. To hurt them! He tried to hurt my friends, so I pushed him. I didn't throw any punches. He punched me!"

"But violence is not the answer, Ace. Are you going to fight everyone that says something bad to your friends? Principal Keller said they are investigating, but I worry.

What if you get suspended? What if you get expelled? You'll have thrown your future out the door," Zzabu said, worriedly.

"I wasn't thinking, Mama," said Ace.

"I know you meant right but I worry that these friends of yours do nothing but get you into trouble. You've left me no choice. Until the school resolves this situation, I want you back home by four. You will neither hang out with those boys nor make any plans unless I have allowed it. I want you focused on your books. I'm sorry, but you leave me no other choice, Ace."

"Understood, Mama," said Ace, sadly. He was powerless and with no friends once again.

* * *

For nearly a week, Ace forced himself to ignore his friends' messages and avoid their usual lunch spot. It was one thing to be trapped in the same detention room with Jamie Bishop, complaining about whatever his parents refused to buy for him, and another thing being away from his new community. During one detention session, Ace had had enough of Jamie's complaints.

"Listen, Jamie. I'd rather listen to a goat sing than hear about how life is so hard for you. I really don't want to talk today," Ace said angrily.

Jamie paused for a minute. "Well, you and everybody else, bro. No one really cares."

Ace turned to him. "Aren't you the popular kid? Everyone wants to be your friend. Why would they not care?"

"I don't know! Everyone keeps talking about you and how smart you are. I see how Ms. Menon listens to you when you raise your hand. Coach Irons even wants to sign you up for next year's soccer team. No one really cares unless I'm pulling a prank or making fun of a nerd," Jamie replied.

"Why can't you just be nice for a change? Why do you have to make someone feel bad for you to feel good about yourself?" asked Ace.

"I don't know," Jamie repeated.

"Yes, you do!" Ace snapped.

"T–th–that's the only way I know how to make friends … okay? I have to be tough. That's what my dad says. If they see me cry or watch nerd stuff, they'll push me around. They'd laugh if I told them I listen to Taylor Swift all day. If people knew who I am, they wouldn't want to be my friend," Jamie explained.

Ace sighed. "Those aren't real friends, Jamie. If you can't be your real self around those people, is it worth it? Maybe you need some new friends. A real friend would tell you that because they care."

"Maybe … Maybe I do … I kinda wish someone would do for me what you did for your friends in the gym the other day," Jamie said.

Ace nodded. "There's nothing stopping you from doing the right thing, Jamie. Maybe one day we can hang out, when you're ready."

"Baby steps, dude. I don't want people thinking I got soft in detention. But you're a cool guy, and smart, too. Sorry about the bruise, bro."

"All good, man. I feel better that I met the real you," said Ace, fist-bumping Jamie as a gesture of reconciliation.

* * *

At the end of the week, Olive burst into Ace's room breathless, like she'd run a marathon.

"A ... Ace!"

"You keep breathing like that and all the oxygen will be used up," said a moody Ace. "What's wrong?"

"Mom ... She just ... got off the phone with Principal Keller and ... guess what? They're not suspending you!"

"What?"

"They didn't like that you pushed that boy Jamie, of course. They've let you off on a warning not to fight in school. Supposedly, there were *a lot* of students that wrote to Keller in support of you!" Olive exclaimed.

Ace couldn't believe it. "Students ... wrote to Keller ... for me? Why?"

"Ace, they're people who got your back. Don't ask why.

You're blessed to have friends willing to be there for you. You should give them a call," Olive said with a smile, closing the door behind her.

The news was both shocking and inspiring to hear. Still, the feeling of shame crept in. How could he look at his friends' faces knowing he had ignored and avoided them? What kind of friend leaves his crew hanging after all they've done for him …

Perhaps he didn't deserve such friends, Ace thought. Perhaps he deserved to be friendless and alone.

* * *

By Sunday, Ace had begun feeling like himself again, though the thought of facing his friends, the Misfits, still made him anxious. As he was about to get ready for breakfast, he heard an aggressive set of knocks at the front door.

"Ace, can you get that?" yelled Olive from the kitchen, making what smelled like American pancakes, his favourite. "Mom and I have our hands full here!"

"Yeah, yeah," Ace replied. As soon he opened the door, King jumped into the house and pounced on him.

"Fam! Where've you been? You ain't picking up our calls or texts. We knew we had to come through!" said an excited King.

He wasn't alone, though. Alongside King was Trivia,

snacking away on a Twix bar, Tower, with a new blue headset on his neck, and two other familiar faces Ace had not expected to see at his home of all places.

"Matilda? Tim? Wh–what … what are you doing here?" Ace finally managed to say.

"Jambo, Ace! Jambo, Ace's family! You have like a really cozy home. Basements aren't my thing, but you guys are totally rocking it. It's, like, so good to see you. Like, how are you, and how's your heart?" Matilda hugged Ace in her yellow winter jacket and brown winter hat.

"I'm … okay … Thanks for asking. I didn't know you all knew each other."

"It wasn't my idea, fam. She has English in the morning with Trivia. She made him spill the beans about your sister's surprise by bribing him with Orange Crush. Weak man, just weak," said King, shaking his head.

"I'm not denying anything. If had to do it again, I would. Besides, Olive clearly said to gather *all* of Ace's friends!" Trivia took another bite of his chocolate bar.

"And you, Tim?" Ace looked over at his spectacled friend.

"Ericksen and I are in the same math class. He told me what happened, and I had to come show my brother from another mother some love. You're the only person that actually greets me and asks me about life stuff. You're real people, Ace. It's just not the same without you!"

Ace, are you going to keep your friends waiting at the door, or are you going to invite them in for some breakfast?" Ace's mother came out of the kitchen and signalled the teens to the dining table.

With their winter gear and shoes off, everyone gathered in the small kitchen and living room for a huge spread of cereal, pancakes, and roasted sausages. The sight of his friends seated next to him, in his home, lit a fire in Ace's heart.

"Ace," Olive said, "we've all been worried about you. I've been worried *sick* about you. Mom and I wanted to do something special for you."

Zzabu walked closer to Ace. "And I want to say I am deeply sorry, Ace. I am sorry for not believing you and keeping you away from your friends. It wasn't right of me, as your mother, to close you off from your community. I was so worried that I wasn't thinking. You friends reached out and shared what you mean to them, how you've made a difference in their lives. I am proud of you. Can you forgive me, my son?"

"Of course, Mama. Of course!" Ace hugged his mother and allowed himself to shed a tear.

"Couldn't you guys come up with a better name than the Misfits?" asked Olive.

"That's because they didn't have me to help pick the name," said Matilda. "Maybe the United Nations? Because we're all from different parts of the world.

I'm pretty sure I'm seventy percent Irish, ten percent Scottish, and twenty percent Italian."

"You wanna cookie for that, Matilda?" King said jokingly.

"You wanna grow a few inches taller and then we can talk, buddy?" Matilda replied, and the whole table burst out laughing.

"Oh, *burn*! Man overboard!" They all laughed for several minutes until Tower started banging on the table.

"Fam, we still haven't told Ace the news."

"What news?" asked Ace.

"Some of the teachers wrote to support you, bro," Tim began. "Ms. Reid, Ms. Menon, and a few of the other teachers went hard and let Principal Keller know that you are one of the standout students of the year. They had your back. Jamie didn't realize this, but he just made you the cool guy of our grade!"

"What? No ... Why would they?"

"That's 'cause you do you, Ace," said King. "You never try to be someone you aren't. You're honest, helpful, and a great friend. I don't know how you do it. I do know that we all got your back."

"Thank you!" Ace cried. "I love you guys!"

"So we still doing the talent show?" Trivia asked.

"Yeah!" said Ace, wiping a couple of tears from his face. "We're still doing it!"

"Before you get carried away, Ace, I also called up a few more people that wanted to speak with you."

Olive went to grab her laptop by the living room couch. She turned on the screen to reveal the faces of Rodney and Ronan from Kampala, waving at Ace and his friends.

Ace looked up at his sister and gave her a silent nod to acknowledge all that she had done, and she did the same, to acknowledge she had his back.

CHAPTER 12
THE RISING STAR

The firewood we gather in our youths is what we will warm ourselves with in old age.

— Nigerian proverb

The day had finally arrived. The moment Ace had been working toward: the New Year Talent show, only a few hours away.

Uncle Jackson and Zzabu in all their excitement had taken Ace to the nearest suit store to pick his preferred suit-and-tie combo for the talent show: a light grey suit and ocean-blue dress shirt. He felt special and important in these colours. He imagined himself looking like a prime minister or president about to deliver a state of the nation address.

Olive knocked on Ace's bedroom door to deliver what she knew was the perfect accessory for his suit.

"Hey, villager, you actually clean up good!"

"You think so? I don't look weird? Give it to me real,

sis," said Ace, anxiously.

"Trust me, everyone's going to be talking about your suit. It just needs one more thing." Olive pulled out an envelope and presented it to Ace. In it was a silvery blue tie, and a handwritten note.

"What's this?"

"Before Dad passed away, he made me promise to give this to you the first day you ever put on a suit. You know Dad. He was all about looking good and fresh for the world. I know he's watching over us and as proud of you as I am."

"Thanks, sis. Except … I don't know how to tie my own tie. Can you help me?"

And she did. Within seconds, Olive had folded and twisted the tie until it looked presentable for Ace to wrap around his neck.

"There! Now heads will be turning when you walk the school hallways today. Come on, we're going to be late for the streetcar."

"You go on ahead," said Ace. "King and the others are going to meet me here so we can walk to school together."

"What, you got some kind of secret service team walking you to school now? Okay, Mister! Good luck at the talent show. I'll be in the crowd cheering you on." Olive gave Ace a hug and ran off to get her school bag.

Ace closed his door and opened the letter his father had left for him, carefully to avoid tearing the last precious remnants of his father's writing. As he read it, he imagined himself in Kampala seated next to his father, watching the night sky like they normally did after dinner.

Ace-Point!

I have a good one for you. Why don't eggs tell jokes? They'd crack each other up! ☺ Don't act like that didn't make you laugh. I know it did.

I know by the time you've read this letter, I will not be around. There's nothing that hurts me more than not being with you, Olive, and your mom, and seeing us grow as a family. I've learned that there's only so much we can control in life, but that does not mean we cannot and should not live life on our terms.

I want you to know that your mother and I have been work-ing day and night to make sure that both you and your sister can experience all the chances and opportunities we didn't have access to. We want you to thrive. We want you to go further than we ever have. I wanted to leave you with something.

Do you remember the one time we saw a shooting star in the sky and you asked me what it was? Do you remember what I told you? Our ancestors used to call them 'rising stars.' Any star that has flown through the cosmos for us to see it shine must have endured many obstacles. It must have seen and experienced so much in its lifetime that helped it navigate space. More importantly, it was lifted up by the many stars that came before it.

Ace, I know the journey before you will not be easy. It will be filled with all sorts of twists and turns, ups and downs, and endless obstacles. There will be sad moments as well as happy ones. But like the stars that shine above us, use every obstacle and every moment as a lesson. Lift others up as they lift you. Pave the way for not only our family, but the many others walking their own path. We owe it to the community that has helped us grow.

You are going to shine, my son. You are going to climb the highest peaks, inspire others, and make your family and I proud. You are our rising star. Don't let anyone tell you otherwise.

I love you with all my heart.
Dad

* * *

Ace placed his father's note in the inner pocket of his suit jacket as his good luck charm, then kissed his mother goodbye.

When he opened his front door, five teenagers stood by the steps of his basement apartment: King, Trivia, Tower, Matilda, and Tim. They too were dressed up and happy to see their friend. As Ace walked up the steps to greet them, he knew that the talent show would be the first of many triumphs — both for him and his fellow rising stars.

"You guys ready to kick it?" asked Ace.

"Lead the way, Ace-man!" said King.

And so he did. Ace led them through the school hallways all the way to the busy stage. As everyone got into position, Ace looked into the crowd of faces. He saw his sister, Olive, waving excitedly. He saw his teachers, Ms. Reid, Ms. Menon, and Coach Irons, all throwing their thumbs up in support.

There was a moment of tension before Ace began, when he heard a voice boom from the back: "Show them what you've got, Ace!" It was Jamie, sitting far from the crowd of popular kids and nodding in acknowledgement.

"I got this!" Ace whispered to himself. He saw the Misfits and gestured to them. Then he began his speech.

No sooner had he said his final words than the entire school came to applause, with the Misfits jumping in joy and Trivia break-dancing on stage. Ace had done it!

Soon, they would enjoy some ice cream, but that didn't matter. He held his head high with joy, knowing now what he didn't know just a few months before: *the sky's the limit.*

AUTHOR'S NOTE

My love for storytelling and writing was inspired profoundly by my late grandmother, Nusula Nsereko. She lived a full life providing for children and grandchildren. She survived in spite of Uganda's civil and political conflicts, which saw the loss of many friends. Even in all the chaos, she never once took for granted the power and voice of the local journalist. The pen of the journalist shines light on the concerns of the day, cuts through the lies, and reveals the secrets the powerful would rather stay in the shadows. Journalists are a pivotal pillar of any democracy and essential for holding our institutions and decision-makers accountable.

ACKNOWLEDGEMENTS

The characters and stories that this novel is based on would not have been possible without the many friends and family who graciously shared their own journey of immigrating to Canada and navigating this country we now call home. Special thanks to my mother, Berti Nsereko Kawooya, for all the sweat and tears and getting us through it all. To the finest sisters in the world, Sheila, Tessa, Lisa, and Tina, to whom I owe all my successes in life. To my amazing brother, Daudi, for having my back and a source of support.

This book would also not have been possible without my community in the city I now call home: Abdi Hersi, Andrew Do, Jackie Wilson, Atul Menon, Christopher Villegas Cho, Amy Ding, Gurion De Zwirek, Bar

Cohen, Ankit Nir, Mia Nguyen, Molly Thomas, Melanie, Thomas, Emily Mills, Alyse Kennedy, Ryerson Maybee, Katrina Grinchak, Gail Wong, Ralf Hensel, Fazilla Almeida, Junaid Lohan, Kim Webb, Denise Brzakala, Rubi Sharma, Sameer Lal, Ornella Harris, Christopher Weir, Shweta Bhatia, and so many more.

Finally, to my editor Allister Thompson, who took a chance on me and continues to push me to be the best writer that I can be, thank you for your patience, diligence, and making the time and space to welcome my stories.